First Day of the School Holidays

Pralene Mahabir

Published by

MELROSE BOOKS

An Imprint of Melrose Press Limited
St Thomas Place, Ely
Cambridgeshire
CB7 4GG, UK
www.melrosebooks.co.uk

FIRST EDITION

Copyright © Pralene Mahabir 2013

The Author asserts her moral right to be identified
as the author of this work

Cover design and illustrations by Jack van Beek

ISBN 978-1-908645-36-4

Printed and bound in Great Britain by:
Short Run Press Limited,
25 Bittern Road, Sowton Industrial Estate
EXETER, Devon, EX2 7LW

FSC
www.fsc.org
MIX
Paper from
responsible sources
FSC® C014540

For my children, Trishara and Nirvaan,
Mummy loves you …

For Kamseelin, my inspiration and my strength, this is the
dawn of another journey together … let's enjoy the ride.

For my mum, dad and my brothers, this is a special book
dedicated to the "good ol' days" as we knew it.

'Good morning, kids,' said Mum, with excitement. 'It's the first day of the school holidays.'

As Mum opened the door, Rhysher, their pet dog, ran in and jumped onto the bed.

'Good morning, Mum,' squealed Trish and Nir in unison, still rubbing their eyes and stretching out on their bunk beds. They then both hugged and played with Rhysher, pulling on his ears. He loved that.

'Time to brush your teeth and wash for the day,' said Mum. 'See you downstairs in fifteen minutes. Breakfast is almost ready. Daddy has already gone off to work!'

As Mum closed the door, Nir and Trish both jumped out of bed and ran into the bathroom. They loved brushing their teeth. Lots of toothpaste and 'brush, brush, brush'. Rhysher ran along with them. He loved toothpaste too, and the kids loved sharing it with him.

After washing, they got into their favourite clothes. Trish put on a pink, polka dot dress with lavender pumps, while Nir put on some white shorts and a delightful red and white striped T-shirt.

Trish, Nir and Rhysher then raced downstairs for breakfast.

When they saw the table, they both licked their lips with delight. They loved breakfast. It was, as Mum had always taught them, the most important meal of the day.

Today breakfast included toast, boiled eggs, cereal and Rooibos tea, the kids' favourite. As they ate, Mum asked, 'What would you like to get up to today, kids?'

'I want to tidy my room first, Mum, and then maybe ride my bicycle outside,' said Trish.

'Very good idea,' replied Mum. 'You can do that after you clean your room. Please help me with the laundry first, and then go play outside.'

'All right, Mum,' said Trish, rolling her eyes as she carried on eating her strawberry cereal with warm milk. She did not like helping Mum with the laundry.

Nir, who had been eating his chocolate cereal with gusto, got up quietly and took his cereal bowl to the sink.

'Not so fast, young man. What are *you* getting up to today?'

'Oh Mum, I just thought that I could play outside, and I promised Mr. Stone next door I would help him mow the lawn. And I want to play fetch with Rhysher,' explained Nir excitedly.

'Oh, no you don't! I suggest you help your sister tidy up first, and then help Mr. Stone,' said Mum in a high pitched voice.

Nir shrugged his shoulders. 'Okay, Mum. Come on, Trish, let's get our chores done first, and then we can go outside to play.'

Both Trish and Nir ran up the stairs. Mum could hear all kinds of noises from pillow fights to shuffling. She smiled and thought to herself, 'The first morning of the holiday is at least off to a good start!'

Trish and Nir started cleaning their room, stopping for a few pillow fights in between, with Rhysher at their heels. Cleaning up was not much fun but had to be done!

'Woof! Woof!' barked Rhysher as the kids were fighting with their pillows. He wanted to play too!

'Kids, clean your room! No pillow fighting. I can hear you!' shouted Mum from downstairs.

The kids quickly realised that the sooner they cleaned up, the sooner they could play outside. They quickly tidied up and ran downstairs, Rhysher in tow.

'All done, Mum!' called Trish. 'I'm ready to help you with the laundry now.'

'Thanks so much, Trish. Go down to the laundry room and start sorting out your school socks. I will be down in a minute,' said Mum.

'Nir!' she called. 'Be careful while you are outside.' Nir was out of earshot by now, but Rhysher barked in reply, 'Woof!'

By lunchtime, Mum and Trish had finished the laundry and were ready to have something to eat. Mum had made the kids' favourite of macaroni and cheese, with a salad.

When they came up from the laundry room, Mum and Trish found Nir - already ravenous - had begun eating his salad, while Rhysher was enjoying the baby tomatoes Nir was sharing with him.

'Good boy,' said Mum, 'you've helped yourself. Here's some macaroni and cheese for you.' And she dished up a plate of steaming food for him.

'Thanks, Mum,' said Nir. Trish sat down and began eating too. 'Yummy, it's delicious as always, Mum,' she said.

'Did you help Mr. Stone mow the lawn?' asked Mum.

'No,' replied Nir. 'He had to take Mrs. Stone to town today. I will help him tomorrow.'

After lunch the kids played in the garden. They had lots of fun playing with Rhysher, and climbing up into their tree house.

Mum relaxed outside on the verandah with a good book, watching them. 'Three more weeks of school holidays,' she sighed. 'This is going to be lots of fun.'